Voyage of the *Jaffa Wind*

A Magical World Awaits You
Read

Voyage of the *Jaffa Wind*

by Tony Abbott

Illustrated by David Merrell

Cover illustration by Tim Jessell

A
LITTLE APPLE
PAPERBACK

SCHOLASTIC INC.
New York Toronto London Auckland Sydney
Mexico City New Delhi Hong Kong Buenos Aires

Book design by Dawn Adelman

ISBN 0-439-30607-8

12 11 10 9 8   4 5 6 7/0

Printed in the U.S.A.   40
First Scholastic printing, February 2002

For my father,
whose voyage was a good one
(1922–2001)

Contents

One

Follow the Spinning Ball

"Kick the ball! Kick it now!"

Eric Hinkle was running on the soccer field at school when a light flashed behind his eyes and he stopped dead.

"Kick it, Eric!"

Eric knew the soccer ball was coming his way, but it didn't matter. He was having a vision.

When he closed his eyes, he saw a

small glowing red ball spinning around inside his head.

He had seen that ball before.

It was called the Ruby Orb of Doobesh.

And it came from Droon.

"Eric-c-c-c!" called his friend Neal.

Droon was the world of amazing creatures and astonishing places he and Neal and their friend Julie had discovered under his basement.

One of the first people they met in Droon was Keeah. She was a very cool princess and amazing junior wizard. Then there was Galen, the five-hundred-and-forty-three-year-old first wizard of Droon. And Max, the funny spider troll.

Zzzz-zzzt! The Ruby Orb spun faster and faster in Eric's mind. He remembered how they had discovered the Orb on their last adventure in Droon, and how Galen had said he would study it in his magical workshop.

In fact, Droon was a land filled with magic and wonder. It was a world of strange secrets and mysteries. A realm of endless excitement and danger!

"Watch out! They want the ball!" Neal cried.

Most of the danger came from a sorcerer named Lord Sparr. He was wicked beyond belief. With his chubby, red-faced Ninn warriors, Sparr wanted to conquer Droon for himself.

Zzz. . . . The Orb was beginning to fade now and as it did, Eric heard a dull cheering noise behind his back.

"Oh man, will you stop *dreaming*!" Julie yelled.

That was just the problem. It was harder and harder for Eric to stop dreaming. Because when Keeah once used her wizardry to save his life, Eric accidentally became a wizard, too.

Yes! A wizard! With magical powers! Well, a few.

"So far," he mumbled, "I can speak into people's brains, make my fingers spark, see weird visions, and make jelly doughnuts appear. I can even send lightning bolts around —"

"But you can't win a game," shouted Julie, running to him. "The other team just tied it up!"

The spinning Orb had faded completely. When Eric blinked and looked downfield, he saw the other team jumping up and down.

"Never mind the game," he told Julie. "We've got to get to Droon right away. I just had a vision —"

Neal rushed over. "There's a minute left

before halftime. Could we at least break the tie?"

Eric looked at his friends. He grinned. "Why not? A little silent teamwork might do the trick!"

The play began with Julie kicking off. She passed the ball to Eric.

Neal, move left! Eric said silently to his friend.

Hearing the words, Neal drifted left just as Eric passed the ball to him. Neal stopped it under his foot and dribbled it downfield.

Eric grinned. "It's working...." He turned to his right. *Julie, go all the way down the other side. Neal, pass it back to me. I'll shoot to Julie.*

Neal doubled back, dodged two red uniforms, spotted Eric in the open, and shot the ball to him.

Eric dribbled it forward, then turned.

Julie, here it comes! Ready ... now!

She shifted to the right as Eric's kick sailed through a gap in the other team straight to her. *And in!*

Julie blasted the ball.

Wham! It shot straight to the net for the score.

"Yes! We lead!" cheered Neal, jumping up and down as the referee blew the half-time whistle.

"We'll be back in a minute!" Julie called out.

"And we *will*, too," Neal added. "Adventures in Droon don't take any time at all."

"Let's go," said Eric.

In a flash, they were across the school yard and through several backyards to Eric's house.

Racing through the kitchen and down to the basement, the three friends quickly pulled away some boxes hiding the closet under the stairs. Julie opened the small door and they crowded in.

Eric turned. "You guys, I know I used my powers a little, but we were pretty awesome out there today. It's all about teamwork."

Julie nodded. "We definitely are the best. Well, at least pretty good!"

"So let's have an adventure!" Neal hit the light. The room went dark for a moment, then —

Whoosh! The gray floor became the top step of a staircase. It shimmered in a rainbow of colors.

"I always get chills when that happens," said Julie. "I wonder what Droon will be like today."

Eric grinned. "There's only one way to know."

Together, the three friends went down the stairs, clinging to the railing on the side.

As they did, the sky below lit up with bright fireworks.

Poom-pa-poom!

Pink-and-blue explosions filled the air.

"Hey, someone's having a party!" said Neal. "I wonder if they heard about our last awesome goal."

The staircase circled down over the calm harbor outside a great walled city.

"Jaffa City," said Eric. "Keeah's hometown."

"And there's her boat," said Neal, pointing.

"It's a ship — not a boat," said Julie. "I'm pretty sure."

Bouncing lightly in the sparkling water was the *Jaffa Wind*, Keeah's royal sailing vessel. It had broad sails, a blue smokestack, and two wings sweeping back from the front to the rear. The kids had sailed on it once before.

"Hello, friends!" sang a small voice from the deck. Friddle, the frizzy-haired royal inventor, waved the children over from the staircase.

"The ship is so beautiful," said Julie.

"Boat," said Neal. "The boat is beautiful."

Friddle blushed a deep red. "You are too kind. But swift as a falcon, she is, with not only sails, but a steam engine and oars. Truly, she is a fine oceangoing vessel, if I do say so myself!"

"I'd like to take a cruise someday," said Eric.

"Me, too," said Neal. "As long as there's plenty of food on board."

"It happens that the king and queen will take just such a cruise around Droon!" Friddle said. "Everyone wants to see the queen after so long."

For years Keeah's mother, Queen Relna,

had been cursed to wander through Droon changing from one animal shape to another. Now the curse was broken and she was back to her normal self.

"Up here!" called a familiar voice. The kids looked up. Leaning out of the highest window of Galen's nearby tower was Princess Keeah, wearing her bright golden crown. Max, the spider troll, sat next to her, waving two of his eight furry legs.

"Come up!" Max chirped happily. "Come!"

Saying good-bye to the busy Friddle, the children rushed to the tower.

Galen's workroom at the top of the tower was cluttered with all sorts of odd-looking magical objects, curled maps, rolled-up carpets, thick old books, and stack upon stack of yellowing paper.

"I love this place," said Neal. "It's the only place messier than my room at home."

"What are all these papers?" Eric asked.

"My master is writing his history of Droon," Max said, scampering to a bookcase and pulling a small brown pot from the highest shelf.

"*The Chronicles of Droon* by Galen Longbeard," said Julie, reading the title page. "I guess being five-hundred-and-forty-three years old, a wizard has lots of stories to tell."

"And more every day," said Max. "Soon Galen and I will hunt gizzleberries in the woods. He loves my gizzleberry pie. It's quite tasty and fat free!"

On Galen's worktable, Eric spotted the glossy red ball he had seen in his vision. "I saw this in my head today," he said, turning to Keeah. "It was spinning all around. I don't know why."

"The Ruby Orb of Doobesh is very old," said Keeah. "No one knows what its purpose is, except that Sparr was going to use it for something. I've been reading Galen's papers, but I haven't found anything about it yet."

"Look," chirped Max, hanging out the window. "There they are!"

The children rushed to the window. The courtyard was filled with people who had come to see their king and queen off on their cruise.

Keeah's father, King Zello, stepped proudly from the palace. Zello was a warrior who always wore a helmet and carried a club, but he was also a kind man.

Next to him strode Queen Relna in a long silver gown. Like Keeah, her blond hair was encircled by a narrow gold crown.

Galen himself stood behind them, wearing his tall hat and blue robe covered with silver moons.

"The queen is radiant!" sighed Max,

leaning out next to Keeah. "And look what I've made her — a scarf! I wove it myself."

He gave Keeah the brown pot, then pulled from it a long colorful scarf. It was woven with a complex pattern of colors and textures, from thick deep blues to fine bright yellows.

"It's really beautiful," said Julie.

Max blushed. "One hundred percent spider silk," he said. "I was quite a weaver in my day. Hats, coats, everything. Now, a box for it!"

When Max spread the scarf on the table to fold it, he accidentally sent the Ruby Orb rolling off the table. But instead of falling to the floor, the Orb floated slowly up to the ceiling.

And it started to spin.

"Hey, look!" said Eric. "That's just like my vision . . . but . . . oh, my gosh!"

Without warning, the red Orb began to

flash. Then it hissed and sparked as if it were alive.

"Wh-wh-what's . . . happening?" Max stammered.

Before anyone could make a move, the red Orb shot out a stinging beam of light. It struck Max on the nose and his orange hair flew straight up.

"Whoa, Max," said Neal. "You're getting . . . um . . . smaller . . ."

"But I'm small enough already — oh, dear!"

Max was shrinking. His legs, body, and face grew smaller and smaller until he was no larger than a mouse.

Max squeaked in fear. "Oh! Help! Fetch Galen quickly. Tell him I — I — oh!"

An instant later — *thluuurrrp!* — Max was sucked right *into* the spinning Orb.

"Max!" Keeah screamed. "Max!"

But the spider troll could not answer.

The Orb spun around the room, then shot out the open window. It circled the courtyard three times, then raced across the sea, where it vanished into the dazzling light of dawn.

Two

Friends and Foes!

Keeah dropped the pot to the floor with a thud. She gaped at Eric. "What should we do?"

Eric felt as if his blood had turned to ice and his legs to stone. He couldn't speak. Max's chatter, which moments before had filled the room, was suddenly gone. Now only silence remained.

Blam! The door of the tower room burst open and Galen stormed in with Friddle. "Max? We're all waiting for you — Max?" He looked around, his eyes widening in terror. "Where is Max? "

"The Ruby Orb," Julie said. "It just . . . took Max away!"

Galen stared out the tower window, then thundered, "Max — stolen by the Orb of Doobesh? This is a spell of Lord Sparr!"

All at once, Eric felt that strange sensation of light flashing in his head. Then he saw something. He slumped to the floor. "I . . . I . . . see him . . . yes . . . It's Max —"

"Tell us!" Galen said, leaning close as if he wished to see the vision himself. "Eric, tell us everything you see."

"Max is inside the Orb," said Eric, his eyes shut tightly. "There are waves . . . the ocean . . ."

"Is he hurt?" asked Keeah.

Eric shook his head. "No, no. But he's

traveling very fast. I can't tell where . . . or why —"

The images in Eric's mind flickered and disappeared. "Sorry," he said. "That's all."

"So," Galen muttered. He took a deep breath and turned away from Eric. "Max, kidnapped. Thirty years we have been to-gether . . . ah, me!"

Keeah grasped the wizard's hand. "We'll find him. We'll cross all of Droon if we have to!"

Friddle jumped. "My princess, if I may suggest, the *Jaffa Wind* is ready for such a voyage."

Galen flicked away a tear and nodded sharply. "So be it. We shall assemble the best crew in all of Droon. And we shall find our Max!"

The great celebration in the city was put aside.

Instead, Queen Relna and King Zello

ordered preparations for the voyage to be made at once.

It was decided that Galen would captain the crew. Keeah would be second in command. Friddle, the great inventor and builder of the ship, would serve as steersman. Batamogi, the keen-eyed, fox-eared king of the Oobja, who had come for the celebration, would be the lookout in the ship's high crow's nest.

Neal, Eric, and Julie volunteered to help hoist the sails and to shout when they saw land.

When the great ship was ready, King Zello rang the city bells. Everyone met at the dock to wish farewell to the brave crew.

Galen quietly and quickly jumped on board.

"Keeah, be careful," said the queen, hugging her daughter tightly. "Be well."

Zello shook hands with Batamogi, Friddle, and the children. "Find our friend, and hurry back safely to our city, all of you."

"Oh!" said Keeah. "I just remembered something." She scuttled off. A moment later she was back with a bulging sack. "Supplies!"

With that, Galen gave a nod and Friddle shouted, "Launch the *Jaffa Wind*!"

The ship's blue smokestack puffed out a big cloud of steam, the sails billowed with wind and, cheered on by the crowd, the *Jaffa Wind* powered away from the royal city.

The morning sun hit the sails and they blazed with color, at first pink and white, then yellow and red, as the wind filled them to bursting.

"Max could be anywhere in our wide world," said Galen, scanning the sea ahead. "Friddle, set a course for Lumpland. We'll ask our old friend Khan, king of the Lumpies, to join our voyage. His nose can sniff danger anywhere."

"Aye, aye!" chirped the inventor. With a turn of the wheel, the ship headed south over the sea. "Roll out the backup sail!"

Following Batamogi, the children quickly climbed the rigging and unfurled the large second mainsail. It bellied full of warm breezes.

Clutching the ropes tightly, Neal found himself smiling. "Is this cool, or what?"

"Definitely, the coolest," said Julie. "It's sure strange how we got our cruise after all."

"It's more like a voyage to rescue a friend," said Eric. He turned to Keeah. "And we will rescue Max. We'll find him. I don't know how, but I know he's okay."

The princess pointed. "Galen is not so sure."

Down below, the old wizard stood silently at the bow, looking out across the waves. In his hand, he clutched a small version of his magic mirror. Now and again he stared at it.

Keeah sighed. "I was reading some of his writing. Max and Galen have been through so many adventures together. Galen's heart is broken."

Though the wind was warm, Eric felt a sudden chill. "Let's talk to him. . . ."

Both of them clambered down the rigging and edged over to the wizard.

"Galen," said Keeah.

He did not move.

"What are you thinking about?" she asked.

Without taking his eyes off the rolling sea ahead, the wizard answered, "Gizzleberries."

Keeah and Eric looked at each other.

"I'll be right back," she whispered.

Eric stepped up next to Galen. "I'm sure we'll find Max. Maybe it's part of the vision thing I have. But I'm pretty sure he's okay."

Galen turned to him, the sea spray wetting his cheeks as if it were tears. "But, Eric, we don't know where Max is. I fear Lord Sparr is behind this, but my mirror tells me nothing. I feel helpless. Yes, helpless and powerless and . . . old!"

Eric had never seen the wizard so sad. He had to say something. "But being old is what makes you so terrific. I mean, you know everything! You've been around forever!"

Galen smiled. "Well, not quite forever . . ."

Thud! Keeah was suddenly back, dropping her bulging sack on the deck at their feet.

"Here's what we need," she said.

"Supplies?" asked Galen. "What supplies?"

Keeah opened the sack. It was full of papers. "It's your history of Droon!" she said. "Maybe there is something about the Ruby Orb in here. Something long ago that maybe you forgot. Something that will help us find Max."

The wizard looked at the papers, then at the children. He suddenly blinked and threw his arms around them. "Yes! My *Chronicles!* There must be something! By gosh, you are right!"

At that moment, Neal shouted, "Land ho!"

"Hey, I'm supposed to say land ho," said Julie. "Land ho!"

The high white bluffs and sandy beaches told them they had reached the shores of Lumpland, home to Khan, king of the purple Lumpies.

Galen breathed in the fresh air, suddenly himself again. "Keeah, you and the others find Khan, and tell him what has happened. In the meantime, I shall pore over my papers. We will find a way to save Max — oh, yes, we shall!"

Keeah and Eric were the first to jump down the landing planks and cross the beach to the rolling dunes of Lumpland. Not far away they spotted a little pillow-shaped creature, riding a shaggy, six-legged pilka.

It was Khan himself, his many-pointed crown perched nobly on his head. As soon as he saw them, the king of the Lumpies slid off his saddle and ran over. "Welcome, my dear friends! I'm just on my daily patrol!"

"The Creepy Orb of Doobesh has kidnapped Max," said Neal. "He's lost. You gotta help."

Khan stood there, his legs wobbling in the sand, speechless. Finally, he sputtered, "Our little Max? Brave weaver and pie maker? Gone?"

Keeah nodded. "We don't know where, but with your help, Khan, we can find him."

"Mostly we need your nose," said Neal, "because it can sniff out danger and evil and stuff."

"And since we're pretty sure Sparr is involved," said Eric, "there'll probably be busloads of danger. And a whole big bunch of evil."

The Lumpy king nodded firmly. "Of course you shall have my help." He pulled several bulging leather pouches off the pilka. They had spouts at one end. Khan popped one open and sniffed. "Good," he said. "Let us go."

"What do you have in there?" asked Julie.

Khan grinned, then held the leather pouch over his mouth and squeezed it. A thin stream of dark juice ran straight into his mouth.

"Gizzleberry juice," he said. "It stains terribly. But it's the favorite drink of Lumpies on the go. Besides, it's what makes us so purple —"

He stopped. His round plum of a nose began to twitch. "Aha!" he whispered.

"What is it?" said Keeah.

Khan jerked almost completely around. "I smell . . . danger! And not on distant shores. But nearby! Right here in fact! Follow me! At once!"

With many little strides, Khan scurried up the side of a giant sand dune and carefully peered over. "So . . ."

Holding a finger to his lips, he waved the children up to him. "Already our adventure begins. Look what we find in my own backyard."

He pointed out across the rolling desert. Next to a grove of palm trees was a crooked red tent.

Khan knew about red tents.

So did the children.

Red tents meant only one thing.

Ninns.

Three

The Crew Gets a Little Bigger

"Ninns!" Eric hissed between his teeth. "What are Sparr's warriors doing in Lump-land?"

Khan grunted. "That's what I'd like to know."

"When Sparr went into hiding, the Ninns scattered everywhere," said Keeah. "If Sparr is behind what happened to Max, we'd better find out what they are up to."

So the five of them — Keeah, Neal,

Julie, Eric, and Khan — padded carefully across the sandy dunes. When they were in the shadow of the palm trees, they heard a snuffling noise from the other side of the tent. Three flying lizards with saddles were lying outside the tent, their long necks stooped to a pool of crystal-blue water.

"Groggles," whispered Khan. "As nasty as the Ninns who ride them. They're thirsty, which means they've been traveling. Better steer clear."

As the children crept closer, they heard someone humming a tune.

Keeah frowned. "Ninns don't hum. They grunt. There must be someone else in there —"

Fwap! The tent flaps burst open and a wild bundle of arms and legs and fur came flying out.

"Yeowww!" it screamed as it slammed

right into Neal and Eric, sending them all tumbling into a palm tree.

Just then, the tent flaps opened again.

"Uh-oh!" Keeah's fingertips shot a spray of sparks — *kkkk!* — and the entire crew was instantly swept up to the top of the palm tree.

"Yikes!" gasped Julie, clinging to the trunk.

"Shhh!" said Keeah. "Look!"

Out of the tent poked the snarling red faces of three very large Ninn warriors. Their tiny black eyes darted around. Their big cheeks puffed up.

"Where he go?" grunted the first.

"Ha! I toss him good!" snarled the second.

"Better tell Sparr, Lord of Evil," said the third.

The Ninns made a terrible chuckling noise, then slipped back inside the tent.

Keeah let out her breath and, with another spray of sparks, lowered everyone to safety behind a high dune.

When she did, a small wiry creature tumbled to the sand next to her.

The creature had a friendly ratlike face, with a pointed snout and shiny whiskers. His arms were wiry but muscular. He wore a silky green tunic and slippers with curled-up tips.

He hopped to his feet and bowed low. "Thank you for saving me from the Ninns! My name is Shago, master thief, at your service —" He stopped. He frowned. He grinned. "My word, I know you!"

"And we know you!" said Eric with a start. "We met you in Agrah-Voor, the city of ghosts!"

"So you did," said the thief, grinning so wide his teeth seemed to stretch from ear to ear.

"In order not to become a ghost myself," he said, "I must spend a week each year outside my city. When I'm here, I must practice snitching."

He held up three purses full of Ninn coins. "But only from Ninns, of course."

"Of course." Keeah raised her eyebrows, then checked to see that she still had everything.

Speaking softly, the children explained why they were there, each adding details to the story.

Even before they finished, Shago offered his services. "Certainly I will help you find Max," he said. "I shall do it for the honor of Droon!"

"Hush. The Ninns," said Khan, peering over the top of the dune. "They are on the move."

They all watched as the Ninns, grunting and growling, tore down the tent and packed it messily onto the back of one of the groggles. Within minutes, they were flying up into the air, heading over the desert to the eastern lands of Droon.

Khan sniffed loudly. "My nose tells me we haven't seen the last of our chubby red friends."

"That reminds me," said Shago, twisting his whiskers. "Before I was thrown out of the tent, I heard the Ninns grunting about something."

"What did they grunt?" asked Neal.

"It seems that Ninns from all over Droon have been called by Sparr," said Shago. "I didn't hear where. But the sorcerer is cooking up something very big."

"And probably very nasty," said Julie.

"And very evil, no doubt," said Keeah. "We'd better get back to the ship right away. Let's go."

When they arrived on board, Galen

was pacing the deck excitedly, his hands full of papers.

He greeted Shago and Khan, then waved his papers high. "It was right here all along. Back in the dark days of ancient Goll, I came across this Ruby Orb of Doobesh. But I knew nothing of its powers. Now, reading my old stories, I remember what else I discovered."

"What?" asked Keeah, her eyes brightening.

"That the Ruby Orb has a twin!" Galen said. "Yes! It's called the Sapphire Star of Doobesh! And with a simple charm, the two Orbs can be made to seek each other across many miles!"

"Oh, my gosh!" said Julie. "Then this Sapphire Star can lead us straight to where Max is!"

"Exactly!" said Galen. "Except . . ."

"Except what?" asked Eric.

"Except no one has seen the Sapphire Star since the end of the Goll empire," said Batamogi, scratching his ears. "And Goll was destroyed four hundred years ago —"

"Ahem . . ."

Shago, who was at that moment leaning against the mast, began to buff his fingernails on his tunic and chuckle softly. "I say . . . *ahem!*"

They all turned to him.

"Yes, Shago? What is it?" asked Keeah.

"I was just thinking how lucky it is that you enlisted me for this little voyage," he said. "For I happen to know where your Sapphire Star is!"

Galen's face lit up. "Shago, you master thief, you! Tell us what you know! Where is the Star?"

The thief grinned with excitement. "The Sapphire Star of Doobesh is locked up on the island of Mikos. In the treasure

house of Bazra, Queen of Robbers. An old enemy of mine, I might add."

"Bazra!" sighed Batamogi. "I've heard of her. She steals from everyone and locks up the treasure in her fortress. No one has ever gotten in!"

Shago coiled his whiskers. "My dear sir —"

"And her guards have two heads!" said Khan. "Two *dog* heads! And they growl and bark and carry spears with lots of blades on them! We'll never get into her fortress, never —"

"My dear sir!" Shago said, wiggling his fingers in the air before him as if he were playing an imaginary instrument. "*You* would never get in. But I am here to show you how!"

Everyone stared at him in awe.

Shago pretended to yawn. "Now, unless you wish to praise me some more, I suggest we go!"

With no more discussion, but with lighter hearts, the crew took their places. Batamogi rushed to the top of the mast with Khan. Eric, Neal, and Julie clambered up the rigging and let down the sail. Galen took position on the bow.

"And we're off!" the wizard cried.

At that, Friddle leaped to the wheel and in a flash the *Jaffa Wind* was on a course for the island of Mikos.

And the treasure fortress of Queen Bazra.

Four

Treasure and Something Else

The sun was just going down when they spotted the rough gray cliffs of the island of Mikos.

Eric watched icy waves break over the rocks. "Not a very friendly place," he muttered.

Keeah wrapped a cloak around her. "Queen Bazra is not a friend to anyone. We'll go ashore under cover of darkness."

"Perfect," said Neal. "That way, nobody can see how scared we are!"

A half hour later, they docked behind an outer bank of high rocks. Friddle and Batamogi kept watch over the ship. Shago and Galen led the others up a twisting path to the top of the cliffs.

From there, they beheld a vast building made of glazed blue stone. Several guards, each with two dog-shaped heads, patrolled the high wall. They wore silvery armor and carried nasty-looking spears.

"Let's not mess with them," Neal whispered.

Shago chuckled softly. "Bazra's treasure house is not open to the public. But it will open for us!"

He crooked his finger and the crew followed him over the rocks and up to the fortress wall.

When all was clear, he untied a rope from his belt and tossed it up. It uncoiled and hung magically in the air. "Don't try this at home," he said, a wink in his eye. "Now . . . follow me!"

One by one, the crew climbed the rope over the wall and onto the roof of the fortress. At each corner stood a tall dragon-shaped tower. Shago scanned the silver rooftop, picking out a small dark spot nearby. "An air vent. We shall enter there."

Suddenly, a fiery light shone down from the towers.

"Searchlights," said Julie. "They'll spot us."

"No," said Galen. Mumbling words under his breath, the wizard raised his hand at the nearest tower. The searchlight blinked and went out. Guards left their posts and ran to the tower.

"I will keep them busy. Go!" whispered Galen.

The crew trotted across the roof. Though it was dark, the roof was still warm from the sun's heat. Eric grinned at Neal and Julie as they made their way to the small opening.

They were all thinking the same thing.

Adventure. That's what Droon was all about.

The opening was just large enough to get through, but was covered by a grate of iron bars.

"We have grates like this in school," said Julie.

"Air vents," Shago said with a chuckle. "To keep Bazra's 'hot' collection well cooled. Khan?"

The Lumpy king pulled a small tool from his pocket. With a few turns he removed the grate.

Lowering his rope into the opening, Shago slid down. The others followed.

It was cool in the fortress, and hushed. The floor was made of large white and black squares.

Shago glanced around. His whiskers twitched. "The main room is straight ahead —"

Khan stuck out his arms. "Wait." He bent to the floor and sniffed. "Walk on only the white tiles. The black ones are booby-trapped. They will sound an alarm!"

Shago grinned. "Good to have you aboard this adventure, Khan." He scampered along the hushed hallways, leaping from one white square to the next.

They passed displays of golden shields, silver helmets, and jeweled necklaces shimmering in the moonlight that streamed through the high windows.

"Nice stuff," muttered Neal. "It's like the art museum my parents take me to."

"Queen Bazra's fortune is built on wealth stolen from others," whispered Shago. "It's time we took some back. Hush now, here we are. . . ."

The room before them was as tall as it was wide and long. Hundreds of tiny silver bells dangled from the ceiling above, waiting for the slightest breeze to disturb them.

"Clever alarm system!" said Keeah.

"Yes, we must be like ghosts here," said Shago. "Ghosts who steal back . . . the Sapphire Star!"

"And there it is," whispered Eric.

In the center of the giant room, basking in a shaft of silver moonlight, was a round crystal ball. It shone deep blue in the moon's light.

"The Sapphire Star!" said Keeah. "It *is*

like the Ruby Orb, only it's blue. Max, it won't be long now —"

Clunk.

Eric turned. "What was that?"

Clunk. Sounds were coming from another, smaller treasure room at the far end.

Julie nudged Eric and Neal. "Let's check it out. If it's guards, we'll come back to warn the others."

"Good idea," said Keeah. "But be careful."

Julie, Eric, and Neal darted across the white tiles to the far room. They heard grunts and thuds coming from inside.

Julie sidled up to the doorway and peered into the dark room. "It's not guards. Take a look."

Inside the small chamber were the same chubby Ninns they had seen in the desert. Two were crouched on the floor while the third was standing on their shoulders, prying something loose from the wall above him.

"Wow," said Neal. "Today must be the day when people steal stuff. Haven't they heard about the dog-headed guards?"

Julie chuckled. "I guess not. Let's go back."

"No," whispered Eric. "We need to see what they're stealing. It's probably for Sparr."

The Ninn on the top was grunting and groaning as he tugged and pulled and wiggled. The thing he was tugging and pulling and wiggling was a giant hammer mounted on the wall. The hammer was nearly as tall as the Ninn himself, and the head of it was the size of a barrel.

As the red warrior yanked on it, the hammer finally came loose. "Ugh . . . oww . . . ooof . . . !"

Crash! The pyramid of Ninns tumbled

to the floor, and the hammer bounced from one white square to another right into the shadows. It stopped an inch from Eric's foot.

"Yikes!" he cried. Without warning, his fingers let out a wild burst of blue sparks.

They lit up the room.

The Ninns jumped back with a grunt. "Children!" Then they put their chubby fingers to their lips. "Shhh! Guards with two heads. Tiny bells. Shh!"

With that, they picked up the giant hammer and tiptoed out of the far end of the room.

Eric gasped. "What . . . what just happened?"

"The Ninns . . . let us go," said Neal.

"Let's get back before they change their minds," said Julie.

The three of them ran back to the main room in time to see Shago lifting the Sapphire Star out of its case. "Aha!" said the thief. "And now we will find our spidery little friend."

"We saw Ninns in the other room!" Julie whispered to Keeah. "They were stealing a big hammer or something. Eric got scared and did the sparky thing with his fingers."

"Uh-oh," whispered Khan. "I see it."

"Uh-oh, you see what?" asked Eric.

"Uh-oh, I see that!" Khan pointed to the ceiling where the last of Eric's sparks was zipping around and around in the air. Finally it flared brightly, then expired, tapping ever so lightly one of the tiny silver alarm bells.

Ding!

Even before the kids could breathe —

Wham! Wham! Heavy wooden doors blasted open, and dozens of two-headed guards in silver armor stomped in.

"Thieves!" barked some of the heads.

"Get them!" barked the other heads.

"Oh, sure!" snapped Neal. "They didn't hear the clutzy Ninns dropping giant hammers all over the place. But the two-heads heard that tiny bell? It's just too weird —"

"Weird or not," said Julie, dragging Neal with her, "those two-heads are coming to get us!"

In a flash, the crew ran to Shago's magic rope. They climbed up, shot out the air vent, and popped out onto the roof.

"Get them!" the rooftop guards growled.

Galen ran to the kids. "Let's not waste our time with spells. I suggest we simply — run!"

With Queen Bazra's dog-headed guards hurling spears at them, the crew of seven ran with all their might back to the ship.

"Friddle!" Galen cried out, his robes flying up behind him. "Get us out of here!"

"Oh, dear, dear!" Friddle gave the ship's engine a jolt just as the crew tumbled aboard.

Vooom! The *Jaffa Wind* jerked and sped out to open sea amid a hail of many-bladed spears.

"Yes! We made it!" cried Eric. "There's teamwork for you!"

Soon the barking of the guards had died away, and the ship was safely speeding across the sea.

"And now to find Max," said Galen. Taking the glassy blue ball in one hand and his papers in the other, the wizard read out an ancient spell. At once, the Orb began to glow, dazzling brightly like a many-pointed star.

"It pulls on my hand!" said Galen. "Go, Sapphire Star, find your twin! And find our Max!"

With that, he tossed the glowing ball

into the air. It hovered overhead for a moment, then — *zzzz!-zzz!-zzzz!* — it whizzed around the ship three times and shot off into the distance.

"After the Star!" cried Keeah.

Instantly, the *Jaffa Wind* crashed high over the waves in hot pursuit.

Five

The Thing About Legends

Twinkling and blazing, the Sapphire Star zipped ever faster across the dark sea.

"The Star is swift!" said Friddle, urging the ship over the crashing waves.

"The *Jaffa Wind* can be just as swift," said Keeah. Smiling, she dug into her supply sack and pulled out the magic harp that had once belonged to her mother. She handed it to Batamogi. "The Oobja are great harp players," she said. "I'll do a spell for a swift voyage, if you'll play."

"Absolutely!" Taking the harp, Batamogi began to strum and sing. His song was of a future time when Droon would finally be at peace. Shago sang together with him.

Keeah murmured softly, and the wind seemed to sing along with them, driving the ship even faster over the waves.

Eric felt chills seeing the magic that Keeah could do. "That's awesome," he said.

"Yes, quite," said Galen, pacing the deck impatiently. "But now that we are under way, what's this I hear about a hammer, hmmm?"

First Eric, then Julie, then Neal told the wizard everything they had seen, describing as much about the hammer as they could remember.

"It was really huge," said Neal. "The

Ninns must be building something really big with it."

"Big and definitely bad," added Julie.

"Hmmpf!" Khan snorted and crossed his arms. "The Ninns are terrible builders. They are far better at destroying things."

Galen stroked his beard slowly. "Quite right," he said. "But I suspect this hammer is neither for building nor destroying. The Ninns are bringing it to Sparr, so its purpose must be a darker one."

"Darker?" asked Keeah, turning to the wizard.

Eric searched the wizard's eyes for a clue. But if Galen knew what Sparr's purpose was, he did not say so. He merely wrapped his robes around him and went back to his pacing.

"He's worried about Max," said Julie. "I mean, what if we lost one another? I don't know about you, but I'd go crazy. Then I'd go find you."

Neal nodded. "Ditto for me. I'd never stop looking until we were all together again. I mean, we can't break up this incredible team, right?"

"Sure," said Eric. He saw the worry in the old wizard's face. But there was something else there, too. Something Galen wouldn't talk about.

Not yet, at least.

Cold waves splashed up the sides of the ship.

"Oh," said Friddle. "That's not good. Look."

Ahead lay two great masses of rocky land. The sea narrowed to a slender channel between them. The Star dipped and entered the channel.

"It's very close up there," the inventor

said. "I worry about the ship running against the rocks."

"We have no choice," said Keeah. "We have to follow it. It's our only way to find Max —"

"Slow the engines," said Galen. "Trim the sails."

While Julie, Neal, and Eric climbed the rigging and tied up the sails, Friddle shut off the engines.

The Star moved slowly through the channel ahead, and the ship drifted behind it. As it passed between the cliffs, the kids spotted bits of wood, planks, rigging, shattered masts, and torn sails clinging to the rocks on either side.

"The remains of busted boats," whispered Neal. "Is this some kind of warning?"

"A warning it is," said Batamogi, turning pale. "There is an old legend about giant bulls that come down to the sea and crush ships on their horns."

"But it's just a legend, right?" said Neal. "Legends aren't true, right? I mean, legends are made-up stories, right? Why isn't anyone agreeing with me?"

"Because of that," said Julie.

Just ahead, the jagged rocks on either side of the narrow passage were carved into the shape of heads. Giant bull heads. Each had three eyes made of bright red rock. Twin horns, all jagged and black, jutted out from each head. The fangs sticking out from each jaw were white granite.

Eric gulped. "I guess the thing about legends is that sometimes . . . they're true."

"The Horns of Ko!" said Shago. "They are nasty heads enchanted by the sorcerers of Goll."

"Enchanted?" asked Julie. "Enchanted how?"

At that moment the bull heads suddenly jerked out from either side of the channel and crashed into each other — *ka-dooom!*

"Holy cows!" cried Neal. "Turn back. We'll be crushed!"

The giant heads pulled apart again. But before long they smashed together once more, sending bits of stone exploding onto the deck of the approaching ship.

"Back up!" said Neal. "This is a warning, all right. We'll take the long way. Map, please?"

"No," said Friddle. "I believe I have a plan. But our sails and steam engine won't help us now. We'll need to row! To the oars, everyone. Row toward the rocks!"

"Toward them?" asked Khan. "But . . . but . . ."

Friddle grinned and took out a pad and pen. "Do as I say. Put your backs into it. And Batamogi, strum that harp!"

As he said this, the rocks pulled apart and the passage was open again.

Slap! Swish! Slap! Swish! Everyone sat in the oar seats and pulled on the oars, as Batamogi took up Keeah's harp again and strummed it.

Thrumm! Thrumm!

Three more times the giant heads clashed and separated, as the *Jaffa Wind* rowed toward them.

Finally, Friddle waved his pad. "Twenty-seven thrums! There are twenty-seven thrums of the harp between each clash of the Horns of Ko. So after the next clash, we need to row quickly through the channel — in less than twenty-seven thrums — before the next clash of the heads. Or crash, or smash, whatever word you like —"

"I don't like any of those words!" said Khan. "I don't like being wet! If we clash or smash or crash, it's all the same to me. I'll get very wet! And when I'm wet I don't dry out for weeks!"

Galen shook his head. "Let us do as Friddle says. Everyone together now — row!"

Full of fear, but trusting the wizard, the crew did as he said. Julie and Eric sat side by side. Neal and Keeah rowed across from them. Behind them were Khan and Shago. On the far side, Galen rowed alone.

Their arms stretched, their backs ached, but they rowed with every ounce of strength they had. All the while, Batamogi kept plucking the harp in slow, measured beats.

Thrumm! Thrumm!

"Eleven," said Friddle. "Twelve . . ."

Splash! When the rocks pulled apart, a swirling dip in the waves drew the ship toward the opening.

"We're doing it!" cried Julie. "We're almost through the opening! I can see the far side."

She spoke too soon. Icy waves from beyond the rocks sent the ship tipping back between the horns — just as the rocks began to close.

"Our ship will be crushed into toothpicks!" Shago said, his slender arms pulling on the thick oar. "Toothpicks for mice!"

Friddle stood at the wheel, calmly making notes on his pad. "Eighteen, nineteen . . ."

Eric looked to his right. The giant red eyes and black horns of the monster bull were plowing toward the ship. On the left, the other bull was doing the same. "We're doomed!" he cried.

"Twenty-two, twenty-three . . ."

The horns were inches from punching holes in the ship when, with a final thrust of the oars, the *Jaffa Wind* scraped between the thundering rocks.

KA . . . DOOOM-OOM-OOM!

"And . . . twenty-seven!" said Friddle, grinning over his pad. He looked up and sighed.

"Now tell me the truth, my friends — was that so hard?"

Six

Battle on the Black Waves

The sea on the far side of the Horns of Ko was as dark and as thick as oil. Waves crashed and heaved, and the wind gusted from every direction at once.

"This is a bad place for sure," said Shago, folding a blanket around him. "I don't like it a bit."

With the air turning blacker and windier by the moment, Friddle fought to keep the blue Star in sight and the ship following at a good pace.

"My mirror shows nothing. . . ." said Galen. "But perhaps a vision of Max will show him to be well?" He turned to Eric and looked at him searchingly.

Eric felt nervous, all of a sudden. There was no flash of light in his head. He felt normal and regular. But he closed his eyes tight and clenched his teeth to try to make a vision come to him.

He tried hard, but it was no use. He opened his eyes. "Sorry, sir," he said. "But I'm sure Max is okay. He's a tough little guy."

Galen breathed in deeply. "Yes, of course."

"We have to be cheerful," said Julie. "And try to look on the bright side, you know?"

Neal glanced up at the gray skies. "Ex-

cept this place is so foggy and dark, it probably never had a bright side!"

"Under the cloak of darkness, much evil
can happen," said Khan.

Eric frowned. "Wait . . . under the cloak
of . . ."

A bright light flashed suddenly behind
his eyes. He shut them tight and saw not
Max as he hoped, but the many-colored
scarf Max had woven for Queen Relna.
The scarf whirled before him, then faded.

Eric staggered and sat on the deck.

"What is it?" asked Keeah, coming to
him.

He opened his eyes. "The scarf. Max's
present for your mother. Why am I seeing
that?"

"Ah!" said Galen. "There is a clue here,
if only we unravel it! A scarf, eh? What can
it mean?"

"I don't know what that means," said Friddle, suddenly jumping to the wheel. "But this means trouble. Look!"

A heavy mist was rolling over the waves. Friddle's slender hand pointed to the sky. "I can barely see the Star!"

"Better slow down," said Keeah.

"Hush! Listen!" said Galen.

Eeee . . . eeeee . . .

"What's going on?" said Julie.

"Is it sea monsters?" asked Neal. "I knew it. Giant bull heads weren't enough, now we have sea monsters attacking our boat —"

"Attacking our *ship*," said Julie.

Eeee . . . eeeee . . . The sound was closer now. And the waters off the side of the ship churned.

Khan scampered to the rail and leaned over. "It sounds like wood creaking."

"And rope straining," whispered Bata-mogi, climbing down to the deck. "It almost sounds like another ship — ooooomph!"

The small king of the mole people slammed to the deck as if someone had knocked him over. An instant later, Shago was tossed into the air — "yeow!" — and flew up into the rigging.

"It's not sea monsters!" Friddle cried. "It's fog pirates! Off the port side! We are being attacked by the fabled . . . fog pirates!"

"Fog pirates?" said Neal. "What are — hey!"

Neal was thrown to the deck. "Who did that?"

"Me!" growled a rough voice.

"Fog pirates are invisible!" said Galen, making jabs in the air with his hands. "On guard!"

There was a low, nasty chuckling sound just before Galen was hurled back into Keeah and Friddle.

All three of them tumbled roughly to the deck.

"Eric, use your fingers on them!" said Julie.

Eric looked around. "Sure, but where *are* they-y-y-yeow!" He was lifted and heaved into Khan. "Ooof!" They were both thrown across the deck.

More unseen boots thumped onto the ship.

"This is so not fair!" said Julie as she was flung against the rigging and bounced across the deck.

"The better for us," growled one invisible pirate. "Come on, mates, take the ship!"

Neal was hurled into the mast, upsetting Khan's bundle of juice pouches. Suddenly, he jumped. "I have an idea!" With his arms full of the leather pouches, he ran back to Eric and Julie.

"Khan's juice!" he said. "It stains —"

"Neal!" said Julie. "We're being attacked by a bunch of see-through pirates and you're — thirsty?"

Khan was thrown over to them. He bounced once, then leaped up. "But Neal's idea is brilliant!" He grabbed a pouch, opened the spout, aimed into the air, and started spraying.

Ssssss! Suddenly, there was a purple pirate standing in front of them.

He had the furry head of a skunk, wore an assortment of rags, and had a patch over one eye.

"I'm wet!" snarled the pirate, wiping gizzleberry juice from his good eye.

"Not half as wet as you're going to be!" said Julie. And with one push —

"oomph!" — the   skunk-headed   pirate went flying over the side.

Thud-thud-thud! Three more fog pirates came swinging over from their ship to the *Jaffa Wind*. This time the crew was ready for them.

Grabbing a juice pouch, Shago flew up on his magic rope and spritzed the pirates from above. "Peekaboo, we see you!" he squealed.

Batamogi, being short, whacked the pirates' knees with stout pieces of rigging. The attackers fell to the deck, sliding on their own wet boots.

"Score three for us!" the Oobja king chirped.

Moving swiftly and deftly, Galen battled four pirates who had tried to take control of the ship's wheel. With one, two, three quick jumps on his feet, he sent the attackers spinning over the side.

"Ah, the smell of gizzleberries in the air!" Galen cried. "I know we shall soon find Max!"

"But Lord Sparr told us to sink you!" growled one pirate as Keeah sent him swinging back to his own ship. "He says you are getting too close —"

"No, fool!" shouted one, who seemed to be the captain. "They aren't supposed to know that!"

"Thank you for the clue!" Galen chirped merrily. "And thank you for a new chapter in my history of Droon! 'Battle on the Black Waves,' I shall call it. Oh, what a victory!"

Friddle turned the wheel sharply, and the *Jaffa Wind* pulled away from the pirate ship.

The wizard cheered as he hurtled one last pirate into the ocean. "You shall not stop us now!"

"We can try!" growled the pirate captain. "Ready, mates. Take aim, and . . . fire!"

Poooom! A fiery ball shot up from an invisible cannon on the pirate ship. It soared in a high arc over the *Jaffa Wind* and struck the Sapphire Star.

"No!" cried Keeah.

The Star wobbled in the air for a moment, then fell through the mist in a swift blue streak.

"Where did it go?" shouted Galen. "Where?"

"Lost at sea!" boomed the captain. "And now, you will be, too. Ready — fire!"

A second *poom* of their cannon sent a low blast over the deck of the *Jaffa Wind*.

Eric saw the fiery ball heading for Julie and Neal. He rushed to them. "Out of the way!"

Then he felt something hot explode

near him. He heard the cracking of wood, and the deck seemed to vanish beneath him.

"Eric!" screamed Keeah.

But he was hurtling down away from the ship.

The crashing waves surged up at him.

And his eyes closed in pain as he struck the black water.

Seven

A Visit to the Big House

Bubbles rushed up at Eric as he plunged deeper into the cold sea. It felt like powerful hands were pulling him under. He couldn't breathe.

This isn't happening! he thought. But the water grew blacker and he sank deeper.

Then light broke across his eyes.

Everything stopped moving and rushing around him. Was he somehow back on the ship?

He looked up. No, this wasn't the ship. He was inside . . . somewhere.

And it was smoky and hot around him.

"Where am I?" he tried to say, but no sound came out.

Then he saw a small figure crouching nearby, his eight legs twitching furiously by a red light.

"Max!" Eric said. "Max! I found you!"

But Max didn't hear him. He was busy weaving a dark fabric of spider silk. It was a cloak of midnight blue entwined with bloodred threads.

Suddenly, Lord Sparr was there. He laid his hands on the cloak, and the red designs sparked and glowed. The cloak seemed alive with magic.

Eric gasped. "A cloak! Sparr wants a cloak! And Max is weaving it for him!"

Someone grabbed his arm from behind. He was pulled back. "Let me go!" he cried.

"Eric!" said a voice. "Wake up!"

He opened his eyes. He was on a sandy beach. Neal was tugging him out of the water. So was Julie. He was soaking wet, gasping for air.

"What . . . what?"

"Those nasty pirate dudes blasted us right off the boat," said Neal.

"Ship," said Julie. "Right off the ship. And into the water. Luckily, we all washed up on some kind of island. Lots of trees and plants and stuff. And you were mumbling something, as if you were dreaming. . . ."

Eric sat up on the sand. "It wasn't a dream. At least I hope not. I think I had another vision."

"I hope not about sea monsters," said Neal.

Eric shook his head, and water came out his ears. "No, a different kind of monster. Lord Sparr. I saw him. And I saw what Max is doing. I know why Sparr kidnapped him."

"Tell us on the way," said Julie. "I spy some lights up on a hill beyond the trees. It might be a house. Maybe they can help us find Keeah and the others and to get back on the ship."

"Boat," said Neal. "I really think it's a boat."

It was nearly nighttime when they made their way from the beach and into the island's thick forest, always keeping their eyes on the lights twinkling atop the hill.

"Sparr is forcing Max to weave him a cloak," Eric said as they trudged through the woods. "And he's loading it up with evil magic."

Neal swatted away the leaves of a large

bush that blocked the path. "Why can't Sparr just go to the sorcerer shop for an extra-large evil cloak?"

Eric shrugged. "I know it doesn't make sense. But why does anybody need new clothes?"

"For school," said Neal. "Whoa. Think of that. Sparr in school. Now that's a scary thought."

"Maybe when you outgrow stuff," said Julie. "Or sometimes you get new clothes for a vacation."

"I got a new jacket for a trip to California," said Neal. "Then I got ice cream on the front —"

Eric gasped. "A trip! A journey! Sparr needs the cloak because he's going somewhere. Somewhere special!"

"Not California, I hope," said Neal.

Julie stopped suddenly. "I don't know

about Sparr, but we just got somewhere. Look."

Before them, on top of the hill, stood a very large house. It was made of wood and had big yellow lamps hanging by the front door.

"Big house," said Eric.

"Big door, too," said Neal, stepping up to it. He pushed slightly on it, and it swung open.

"Big room," said Julie. The single room inside went from the front door to the back. It was almost as big as their school gym.

"Um . . . big table and chairs," Neal mumbled. "Guys, I think we found the house of a . . ."

Thump! Thump!

Eric grabbed Julie and Neal and dived under the table, in the shadows of its long black tablecloth. They watched as a man stomped in.

A big man. A huge man. A big, huge man.

"Boat, ship, whatever," whispered Neal. "I'm sure we'll agree that this guy's a . . . a . . . giant!"

He was a giant. He stood at least thirty feet tall. He wore strange animal skins, colorful furs, and an enormous beard. And he was rubbing his forehead over and over.

"Strange little pea-sized thing," he groaned. "Fell from the sky right on old Num's head!"

The giant held up a small blue ball. "If the thing wasn't so pretty, I'd crush it under my foot, I would!"

"He's got the Star!" whispered Eric. "Yay!"

"Yay?" said Neal. "He's a giant! He'll

crush *us* under his foot. His very, very huge foot!"

"You stay there," Num said, setting the Star on the table and starting for the door again. "I've got to light the lamps for you-know-who!"

With that, the giant stomped out of the house.

"Quick, let's grab the Star and go," said Eric.

Neal gave him a look. "You must have drunk some silly water while you were drowning, Eric. The table is, like, a thousand feet high."

Eric grinned. "Teamwork. You boost me up, then Julie can get on my shoulders. All of us together should be able to get high enough. We'll brace ourselves against a table leg, then Julie can climb the table-cloth the rest of the way."

She shrugged. "I guess it's worth a try."

In a flash, Eric was up on Neal's shoulders. Julie climbed up from Neal's knees to his shoulders, then to Eric's, clutching the table leg for support.

"I still can't reach it," said Julie.

"Try pulling the tablecloth," said Neal. "The Orb might come to you. I used to do that when I was little and my mom hid candy on the table. But I always got it. "

"That explains so much," said Julie. She tugged on the tablecloth. The Orb rolled closer. "It's coming . . . yes! . . . I got it!"

Thump! Num stomped back into the room.

"Oh!" Julie gasped, nearly losing her balance. She clutched the thick black tablecloth and it slid off the table and fell completely over her head.

"Hey, it's dark in here!" Neal gasped.

"Ahhhh!" boomed the giant. "A ghost!

There in the shadows! Come out where I can see you!"

Eric spoke silently to his friends. *Guys, don't make a move. Stay in the shadows. Stay still.*

The floor rumbled as Num took a step closer. "Wait, is it *you* in the dark there? Is it . . . *you*?"

Who does he think we are? asked Eric.

"Is it really you . . . Lord Sparr?" Num asked. "In your long black cloak?"

Eric began to sweat. *Oh, man, I wish I knew a spell that would . . . wait . . . huh?*

At that moment, a strange word popped into Eric's head.

Seku-ta-moto!

"What?" said Julie, her voice suddenly loud and low and sounding exactly like . . .

"Lord Sparr!" cried Num. "It *is* you! Please come into the light."

"Um . . . NO!" said Julie, her voice booming loudly. "I like the shadows!"

This is awesome, said Eric silently. *You sound just like Sparr —*

"Oh, great king of badfulness! Oh, your most low nastiness! You've come to visit poor Num again! Are you checking on me so soon?"

So soon? said Eric. *Sparr must be nearby.*

"You see I have lit the lamps as you wanted, to show your Ninns the way to the mountain," the giant said.

Julie, ask him stuff, said Eric. *We need to find out everything we can about what Sparr's up to.*

"Ah, yes!" snarled Julie. "The mountain. Ha! And what is this mountain again?"

"Why, it's the Mountain of . . . of . . . Kahfoo."

"Bless you!" boomed Julie.

Num scratched his head. "No, I mean it's Kahfoo's mountain, you know the place. . . ."

"Of course I know!" Julie shouted. "I am testing you! What's in this mountain of Kahfoo?"

"The Room of Kahfoo," said Num.

"Very good. And in the Room of Kahfoo?"

"Why, Kahfoo himself, of course."

"Excellent!" boomed Julie. "And now the bonus question. Who is Kahfoo —"

"Oh, Lord Sparr!" Num said. "I'm just so overcome with joy! I can't believe you are in Num's house. And you are talking to me. Just let me just touch the hem of your cloak —"

"No! No!" said Julie.

Neal, back up! cried Eric.

But when Neal stepped back, Num tugged on the tablecloth and — *flooop!* —

it slid completely off the kids and onto the floor.

And there was Num's huge face, looking from the cloth to the kids, then to the cloth again.

Then Num's face got red. "You're not Sparr. You're . . . pixies! You tricked me! And you've got my blue ball!"

In a flash, Eric and Julie leaped off Neal and onto the floor.

"Run!" cried Eric. "Julie, the Star!"

She tossed it to him, and then he tossed it to Neal, and Neal tossed it back to Julie.

"Give it back!" Num yelled. He stomped all over the room as the kids kept tossing the Star away from him.

"Out the door!" said Neal. And the three friends jumped for the door, slid out, and charged down through the woods to the beach.

Num shouted and growled and finally

started throwing rocks at the kids. *Boom! Crash! Thud!*

"Hurry!" said Julie. "Num wants to crush us!"

Eric clutched the Sapphire Star and began mumbling words that popped into his head. "Septo-reema-flimbo . . . septo-reema-flimbo —"

Zzzzzt! The Star shot up from his hand and spun high over his head. It followed the kids down to the beach.

"There it is!" yelled a distant voice. Then came the sound of waves splashing against wood.

"That's Batamogi's voice!" said Julie. "It's the *Jaffa Wind*!"

Thomp! Thomp! Num was getting closer.

"Somebody, help us!" Eric called out.

The ship sailed toward the beach and Keeah, leaning over the side, sent a spray of blue sparks across the water to the island.

It was like a path of blue light. The kids raced across it and plopped down to the deck.

Friddle gunned the engines and the *Jaffa Wind* soared over the waves from Num's island. Num stood on the shore shaking his giant fists at the crew, but there was nothing he could do.

Suddenly — *zip-zip-zip-zip!* — the Sapphire Star soared over the ship, spun around it three times, then shot into the darkening skies of the east.

Friddle jumped when he saw it. "Setting course!" he shouted. "Max is not far away now!"

The wizard nodded, his eyes brightening with hope. "And once again . . . we're off!"

Eight

Big Bad Evil Mountain

The sea foamed behind the great ship as it plowed over the waves.

As soon as he caught his breath, Eric told Galen and Keeah everything that happened. "I think Sparr needs Max to weave him a magic cloak."

"He wants to go someplace," Julie added.

"And it probably has to do with some dude named Kazoo or Tofu or something," said Neal. "Num said he lives in a mountain near here."

Galen brooded silently, standing at the bow overlooking the rushing sea. When he turned toward the children, his face was pale.

"The Mountain of Kahfoo?" he asked.

"That's it!" said Neal. "You've heard of him?"

The wizard breathed in deeply and nodded. "Oh, that I had never heard his name again! I should have guessed long ago, at the treasure fortress. Why, I asked myself, would the Ninns steal a hammer? You have just told me why."

"Tell us," said Keeah. "We need to know."

The ship rolled back and forth over the waves.

Galen nodded. "Kahfoo the Great was, no . . . *is* a snake."

"A snake?" said Khan. "Let me guess. A large snake? If he has his own mountain . . ."

"Very large and very powerful," said the wizard. "He is a beast born centuries ago."

"But we've fought beasts before," said Keeah. "With Eric helping us, there are three wizards right here."

"Sparr seeks Kahfoo not to fight us," said Galen. "He seeks to ride Kahfoo into the very heart of Droon. Into the very underworld of ancient Goll, empire of evil."

Keeah shook her head. "But you destroyed Goll. You wrote about it in your *Chronicles*."

The wizard breathed deeply. He opened his lips, then closed them without speaking. His eyes searched the dark, starless sky, then the rolling sea ahead. No one spoke. Finally, he turned to the children.

"Some things can never be destroyed, only locked away," he said. "In the underworld of Goll lie unimaginable dangers and powers and secrets that Sparr needs to complete his plans."

"But if I remember my nursery rhymes," said Batamogi, "you sealed the giant stone gates to Goll and they could never be reopened."

Galen turned. "Never say never, my friend. There was one device, as old as Goll itself, that had the power to unseal those rocks —"

"The hammer!" said Julie.

"More precisely, the Hammer of Kahfoo," said Galen. "And Kahfoo himself, giant snake, lies behind his gate, waiting to take Sparr to the heart of Goll. Now you see what we're up against."

No one said a word.

Batamogi broke the silence. "As dark as

things seem now, I must direct your attention upward."

Three large swarms of Ninns riding groggles met in the sky overhead. After joining, they flew across the water into the darkness.

"They are bringing the hammer to Sparr," said the wizard. "Let us waste no time."

"We shall be there as soon as we can!" chirped Friddle. He turned the wheel, the engine gave a strong blast of steam, and the ship raced across the open sea.

For one hour, two hours, five hours, they followed the Sapphire Star. Near morning, the Star began to slow.

"It senses its twin nearby," said Khan. "The Ruby Orb is not far away. The Orb . . . and Max!"

A short time later, the Sapphire Star stopped, hovering over a spot off the bow of the ship. Friddle cut the engines. Bata-mogi, Khan, and Shago tied up the sails.

The *Jaffa Wind* drifted to a stop.

Keeah turned to Eric. "I don't like this. The Star isn't moving, but there isn't land for miles."

"I fear there is," said Galen, his forehead a mass of wrinkles. "Four hundred years ago, when the land of Goll was in flames, the earth trembled and rocked. What wasn't buried fell under the sea."

Neal raised his hand. "You mean . . . *this* sea?"

"Exactly."

"You wrote that earthquakes and floods changed the face of Goll forever," said Keeah.

"Changed the face," said the wizard, "but not the heart. I had hoped Goll would be lost forever under the tumbled ground, under the sea —"

The water bubbled and hissed under the Star.

"Something is happening!" said Khan.

"It begins," said Galen. "It begins. . . ."

Before their eyes the water beneath the Star parted with a great splash. The stony crown of a mountain thrust itself up from below the waves.

Its summit was carved to look like the head of a snake with a broad, flat head and fangs that dripped black water.

"The Mountain of Kahfoo!" said Bata-mogi.

The peak rose higher and higher, until it was an entire island of gray stone, glistening in the dawn's light.

Slowly, the *Jaffa Wind* rounded the new island, its crew searching for a way in. The jagged cliffs were dark, eerie, even as the sky brightened.

Then — *kaww! kaww!* — the giant

swarm of groggles massed over the island's carved peak.

"Quickly, Keeah," said Galen. "You and me, a trick borrowed from the fog pirates!"

Together the princess and the wizard blew out a long breath and a thick mist covered the ship, hiding it from the Ninns.

"Ha-ha!" Shago whooped. "Is there nothing our fantastic wizards cannot do?"

Eric wondered about that. Sparr was growing in power. And what about Eric himself? Would he really be able to help Keeah and Galen? Would the three of them together be enough to stop Sparr's plans? Whatever those plans were?

"A cave," whispered Khan. "I see it, there!"

In the side of Kahfoo's mountain was a large, black opening. Seawater splashed and thundered into the opening, then rushed from it, leaving a narrow river of

water flowing into the depths of the mountain.

In a final flourish of blue light, the Sapphire Star circled the mountain three times, then shot into the black hole of the cave and vanished.

"Max must be in there!" said Julie. "We've found him."

"We've found Lord Sparr, too," said Shago.

The Ninns prodded their groggles and the whole army of them swarmed into the mouth of the cave.

"The Ninns go to greet their master," said Galen.

Neal gulped loudly. "So I suppose we'll go in there soon, too?"

"Sooner than soon," said the wizard.

Neal sighed. "I was afraid of that."

Nine

The Room of Kahfoo

The *Jaffa Wind* drifted quietly into the cave until the river became too narrow. Friddle pulled close to the bank and docked the ship.

"Let us proceed on foot," Galen whispered.

Lighting a wand, he jumped from the ship onto a rock. Keeah lit one and showed Eric how to, also. The rest of the crew followed behind.

Together they tramped down a crooked path alongside the river. For a while, the path remained level, then it twisted downward into a damp tunnel beneath the mountain.

After a while, they noticed a flickering light ahead. Creeping closer, they spied a small cave cut into the side of the passage. There were voices coming from it, but not the deep, growly voices of Ninns.

They were chirping and squeaking.

"Oh, my!" said Keeah, hurrying ahead.

Rushing into the cave, they found three spider trolls crouched on the wet floor. Their legs, eight on each of them, were tied with ropes.

"Max!" cried Galen.

A quick burst of light from his fingertips freed the trolls and Max leaped up.

"Master, my master!" he chirped.

Galen flew to him. "Dear friend!"

The two hugged for a long time.

Finally, the wizard drew back, wiping a tear from his cheek. "Well, quite an adventure you've had, eh, my old chum?"

"Yes, indeed!" said the spider troll, his own eyes moist with tears of joy. "I was trapped in that Orb for a long time before it came here. After that it captured more of my troll friends."

"We were forced to weave a cloak of midnight threads, using the terrible runes of Goll as its pattern," said an old troll with bristly gray hair.

"Sparr says its magic will protect him on a long journey," chirped the smallest of the three.

"We know about that," said Neal. "He wants to ride some big snake to the middle of Goll."

Max's eyes bulged. "Oh, dear! But I thought a journey to Goll was impossible!"

Pooooom. The mountain around them shook.

"Sparr is trying to prove otherwise, my friend," said Galen. "That sound is nothing less than the ancient hammer Sparr is using to blast into the Room of Kahfoo! Come, we must go."

"Khan, your nose, please?" said Keeah.

"At your service," said the Lumpy king. He sniffed and pointed. "I smell snake. This way."

As they scrabbled through a series of tunnels, Max told how the mountain surfaced seven times a day, at each of the seven tides.

"I shall calculate the next time," said Friddle. He immediately began scratching on his pad.

Without warning, Shago halted. "I may not have a Lumpy nose, but even I can smell that."

"Ninns," said Julie. "And, phew. It smells like a lot of them. Real close by, too."

Soon the passage opened into a large cavern that was filled with Ninns. Silently, the crew crept into the shadows and watched.

A voice boomed out.

"Ninns, behold! I shall make history, right before your squinting little eyes!"

Wearing a dazzling cloak of midnight blue woven all over with odd designs of bloodred thread, Sparr stepped up to a high wall of rock.

He moved his hands over the rough surface. "Yes, it begins to crack. The Room of Kahfoo is behind this wall. Ninns, this is a great moment in the history of Goll!"

"And a terrible moment in the history of Droon," said Galen, his keen eyes scanning the room. "There are fifty Ninns, at least. My friends, we have a battle before us. Be ready —"

Clasping the thick handle of the hammer, Sparr whirled it over his head once, twice, three times. Then he heaved it at the wall of rock.

Pooooom-oooom! The whole mountain quaked from the force of the blow. And from ceiling to floor, the wall split apart. Its two ragged halves slid away.

Immediately, a fiery light blazed out.

Sparr shielded his face. "At last, at last, I have found you, O terrifying realm of Goll!"

As the walls parted, they saw the hundreds of ruined columns, fallen walls, and broken stones that were the remains of an ancient empire.

But by far the most amazing sight was the giant snake that lay coiled amid the ruins. It gave off a dazzling light as if its scales were on fire. Its great flat head sat staring at Sparr.

"Um . . . I think we found Kazoo," said Neal.

"Kahfoo," whispered Julie.

"Bless you!" said Max.

Behind the snake was a twisted path through the ruined stones far into the shadowy distance.

Sparr strode into the blazing cavern, the jagged V-shaped scar on his forehead turning red in the light.

"Kahfoo the Great!" he cried. "Take me to the heart of the underworld. Let me see its old palaces and temples where old secrets will be revealed to me. It is a path of danger, yet my magic cloak will protect me. I will find what I seek! I will conquer *everything*!"

"Oh, get a life!" whispered Julie. "The guy isn't happy having a bunch of Ninns obey him, he needs everybody else to do it, too?"

Neal snorted. "He definitely has issues."

"Kahfoo . . . arise!" said Sparr.

At his command, the snake slowly lifted its head and began to uncoil, hissing menacingly.

It slithered through the ruins to its full length, stopped, turned its head to Sparr, and waited.

"Enough!" snarled Galen, his fingers sparking. He burst out of hiding and jumped into the cavern. "Sparr — you shall not find what you seek!"

The sorcerer turned. His eyes flashed. "You!"

The fins behind Sparr's ears turned from purple to black. "You cannot scare me, old man. You or your little army. Part one of my plan is already complete —"

Neal growled. "What is your dumb plan?"

"And how many parts does it have?" asked Khan.

Sparr laughed cruelly, then stared right at Eric. "It's nice to know that one of us will help me find my destiny."

"Hold your tongue, Sparr," Galen hissed.

Eric shivered. One of *us?*

Keeah clutched his arm. "Eric, remember that you are not alone. And you will *not* help Sparr!"

In Keeah's face, he saw the strength he had seen so many times before, but it was different now. Somehow, it made him feel strong, too.

A single spark flashed from her hand to his.

"Enough talk," said Galen. "We shall

show you what we are worth — three against one!"

Keeah and Eric jumped to one side, Galen to the other, and together they sent blast after blast at the sorcerer. *Kkkk-boom-boom-boom!*

Sparr wrapped his new cloak around him and backed into the cave. "Ninns, get the children!"

At his word, a squad of the red warriors rushed up to a ledge and began hurtling rocks at Neal and Julie. They ran for shelter while Shago sent his magic rope coiling around the Ninns.

With a quick yank, the Ninns came bouncing to the floor below. Then Max and his fellow trolls swiftly twirled a spider silk net over them.

"Score one for the good guys!" yelled Neal.

Khan and Batamogi together were more than a match for any single Ninn. Friddle, who did not fight, kept score on his scratch pad.

"We are winning!" he said. "Yes, we are!"

"That's because we are one awesome team!" Neal whooped.

With each blast, Sparr edged closer and closer to the giant snake. But even as the kids seemed to gain the upper hand, Eric felt his hands weakening, as if he were growing tired.

"Keeah, something's wrong," he said.

"I feel it, too," she said, fighting alongside him. "Even Galen seems to be tiring —"

The sorcerer laughed. "Yes! Yes! You feel it, all of you. It is the magic of the old empire. The longer you stay in Goll, the

weaker you become. At the same time, I become more powerful!"

He leaped onto Kahfoo's fiery back, protected from the flames by his magic cloak. "So you see, both ways, I win."

"Not always, Sparr!" chirped Max's little voice. "In five . . . four . . . three . . . two . . ."

Whoompf! A tongue of flame leaped from the snake's back and onto Sparr's cloak. The cloak burst into flames. Sparr howled, "But . . . but . . . *how?*"

Max jumped up and down with glee. "I did that! I did that! I wove a little something extra into the cloak. Serves you right for forcing us!"

As Kahfoo slithered into the distance, Sparr tried to put out the fire. "Ooh! Ouch! Ackkk!"

Galen burst out laughing. "Oh, Max!

You have done well. This is one for the *Chronicles*!"

"Ninns!" yelled Sparr. "Follow me! Ouch!"

Blindly obeying their master, the Ninns jumped onto Kahfoo's fiery back, too. "Ooh! Agg! Ackk!" they cried. "The things we do for Sparr!"

Finally, the twin Orbs of Doobesh, spinning around together, followed the snake into the underworld of Goll.

And Sparr cried out his last, strange word.

"*Koo — ko — sah — lah — temm!*"

"What does that mean?" asked Max.

Vrrrt! The giant stone doors began to close.

"I think we know what it means!" said Neal. "And I think we'd better run — now!"

Ten

Into the Underworld

The crew raced from the Room of Kah-foo and slipped through the closing doors. But Galen turned, staring back at the fiery snake.

"Master," said Max. "Let's go, quickly."

Galen shook his head. "Sparr is on a terrible quest. Perhaps I can discover a secret in Goll that will defeat him once and for all. I must follow him. It may be Droon's only hope."

Trembling, Max clung to Galen's robe. "But master . . . you can't leave . . . you . . . you have no magic cloak."

"And you heard Sparr," said Keeah. "You'll lose your powers in the under-world."

The earth thundered and the great black doors inched closer together.

"I have the love of all of you," said the wizard. "What better gift can a person have?" Then, winking, he said, "Besides, there are still some tricks up my sleeve! As for you, your journey lies elsewhere. Your adventure together has just begun. Now don't worry, we'll meet again in the blink of an eye!"

With that, Galen leaped back through the crack of jagged stone. Rushing toward the fiery snake, he jumped onto its back. It twitched and slithered and carried him away, deep into the underworld of Goll.

"Master!" Max cried. "I'll make a great big pie for your return! A huge pie, the best pie —"

A moment later, the doors shut with a resounding *booom*. And Galen was gone.

Everyone stared at the blank wall of stone.

"Oh," Max whimpered. "Oh." His head sank and his legs collapsed beneath him.

Keeah tried to comfort him. "Galen will come back, Max. He always keeps his word —"

Friddle scampered up the tunnel, waving his pad. "I've finished my calculations. The mountain will sink again in . . . three minutes!"

Eric turned to Keeah. "You're captain now."

The princess took a breath. "To the ship!"

By the time they got to the mouth of

the cave, giant waves were surging to and fro, knocking the ship from side to side.

"Aft engines on," cried Keeah. "Set sail. Everyone to the oars. We need as much speed as we can get!"

"Aye, aye, Captain!" shouted the crew.

With only moments to spare, the *Jaffa Wind* cleared the cave.

The instant the ship launched out to the open sea, the giant mountain of Kahfoo crashed completely beneath the waves.

"Hooray!" Max chirped. He jumped into Keeah's arms. "You have saved the ship. You are a great captain. Galen would be proud. Now, let us make a course for home and try to find him!"

"No winds or waves or beasts shall hinder our voyage," said Keeah. "Batamogi, harp, please!"

The king of the Oobja plucked a delicate song on the harp and a blue glow surrounded the *Jaffa Wind*. Its bright sails spread in the morning sun like giant wings, and the ship gathered speed as never before.

From his place in the rigging, Eric looked down at Keeah standing where Galen had stood.

He knew she was probably afraid. He was scared, too. But he remembered what Galen had told them, and he said it aloud.

"Our adventure together has just begun."

Neal grinned. "I love the way that sounds."

"It means we'll all be together for a long time," said Julie. "Keeah, too. That's the best part."

They climbed down the ropes to the deck.

With his mind focused only on his power, Eric sent a single spiral of blue light over to the princess. It lightly tapped her on the shoulder.

Keeah turned and smiled as the three kids approached her.

"We want to help," said Eric.

"A lot," said Julie.

"You are helping," Keeah replied. "More than you know."

The four friends stood together against the railing, looking out over the sea. The sky was a shimmering rainbow of purple and pink and blue.

Four days and nights, they sailed back over the seas toward Jaffa City. On the way, Khan, Batamogi, Shago, and the spider trolls all went back to their homes. On the fifth day, Max sighted the many-colored towers of the royal city.

"Land ho!" cried Neal.

"I saw it first," said Julie. "Land ho, for real!"

When the ship sailed into the harbor, King Zello was there with hundreds of well-wishers.

"Welcome!" he boomed. "You are all safe!"

Keeah tried to hold back her tears as she told him what had happened. "Galen is gone."

Zello broke into a strange smile. "Er, not quite. He's been on his magic mirror all morning, giving us instructions and telling us to help you —"

Max jumped. "Oh, let me see him!"

Queen Relna was waiting for them in the tower when they rushed in. "Everyone, look!"

On the mirror was Galen's face. His white hair was being blown about by a mysterious wind. The air around him was red. There was a terrible crashing and booming noise in the background.

"Max, Keeah, children," said Galen, turning to them, "please sharpen more pens for my return. I shall have much to write in my *Chronicles*!"

"I shall, master, I shall!" chirped Max, sounding very much like his old self again.

"Together," said Galen, "I want you to find something called the Moon Scroll. It will explain everything. Now more than ever, you will need to know the truth. Do not fail!"

"The Moon Scroll," said Eric. "We'll find it."

"Once you find it, you shall begin the adventure of a lifetime," said the wizard.

"As if it's been boring so far," Neal joked.

"We won't fail to find the scroll," said Keeah.

"Just as long as we find you, too!" added Friddle.

"Find me you shall!" said Galen. Then, grinning, he added, "But one more word. Max?"

"Here!" chirped the spider troll.

"We shall have our berry pies, my friend," the wizard said. "But while I am gone, you know what to do, remember? You have the key."

"I do!" the troll chirped, clapping his eight furry feet together. "I shall do it right away."

"Then all is well!" With that, Galen sped away into the noisy distance and the mirror faded.

Queen Relna turned to Max. "What did Galen mean when he said that you have the key?"

Max chuckled. "The key to the tower closet."

"What's in there?" asked Keeah.

Max scurried over to a narrow door in

the wall and from a hidden compartment next to it, he pulled a key. Inserting it into the door, he turned it, and the door popped open.

Everyone gasped.

"Galen?" said Julie.

It was the wizard, or at least a double of him, exact in every detail from his tall blue hat to the curled velvet slippers on his feet.

"Amazing!" said Keeah. "But . . . but . . . why . . . ?"

Max chuckled. "Just a little something my master whipped up for emergencies, so the dark forces of Droon would not think he is gone for good."

"This is wonderful!" boomed King Zello. "It will be as if our Galen is not away at all!"

"A perfect likeness," declared the queen.

Max pressed a jewel on the wizard's

wrist and this new Galen whirled around in the closet, strode backward into the room, did a half flip, and landed on the ceiling.

"Snibble-ibble-flit-blit!" the wizard squeaked. "You are pleased to meet me! Allow me to shake your feet! Good-bye!" With that, he went quiet.

"Um, he seems a little backward," said Neal.

Keeah laughed brightly. "Our pretend Galen is not so perfect after all."

Max's face fell into a frown. "Hmm, I can see he'll need some work. Quite a bit, actually!"

At that moment, the rainbow-colored staircase appeared just outside the tower window.

"That's our cue to go home," said Julie. "We have a soccer game to finish, remember?"

Eric began to smile. "But this team needs to play again, too. So we'll definitely be back."

"Besides," said Neal, "where else could we go on such a cool boat ride?"

Julie grinned at Keeah. "He means ship ride."

"It's called a voyage!" said Friddle.

Laughing together, the three friends charged up the stairs, already wondering about their next adventure in the secret world of Droon.

About the Author

Tony Abbott is the author of more than three dozen funny novels for young readers, including the popular *Danger Guys* books and *The Weird Zone* series. Since childhood he has been drawn to stories that challenge the imagination, and, like Eric, Julie, and Neal, he often dreamed of finding doors that open to other worlds. Now that he is older — though not quite as old as Galen Longbeard — he believes he may have found some of those doors. They are called books. Tony Abbott was born in Ohio and now lives with his wife and two daughters in Connecticut.

For more information about Tony Abbott and the continuing saga of Droon, please visit his website at *www.tonyabbottbooks.com.*

THE SECRETS OF DROON

A Magical Series by Tony Abbott

Under the stairs, a magical world awaits you!

- ☐ BDK 0-590-10839-5 #1: The Hidden Stairs and the Magic Carpet
- ☐ BDK 0-590-10841-7 #2: Journey to the Volcano Palace
- ☐ BDK 0-590-10840-9 #3: The Mysterious Island
- ☐ BDK 0-590-10842-5 #4: City in the Clouds
- ☐ BDK 0-590-10843-3 #5: The Great Ice Battle
- ☐ BDK 0-590-10844-1 #6: The Sleeping Giant of Goll
- ☐ BDK 0-439-18297-2 #7: Into the Land of the Lost
- ☐ BDK 0-439-18298-0 #8: The Golden Wasp
- ☐ BDK 0-439-20772-X #9: The Tower of the Elf King
- ☐ BDK 0-439-20784-3 #10: Quest for the Queen
- ☐ BDK 0-439-20785-1 #11: The Hawk Bandits of Tarkoom
- ☐ BDK 0-439-20786-X #12: Under the Serpent Sea
- ☐ BDK 0-439-30606-X #13: The Mask of Maliban
- ☐ BDK 0-439-30607-8 #14: Voyage of the *Jaffa Wind*

$3.99 each!

Available Wherever You Buy Books or Use This Order Form

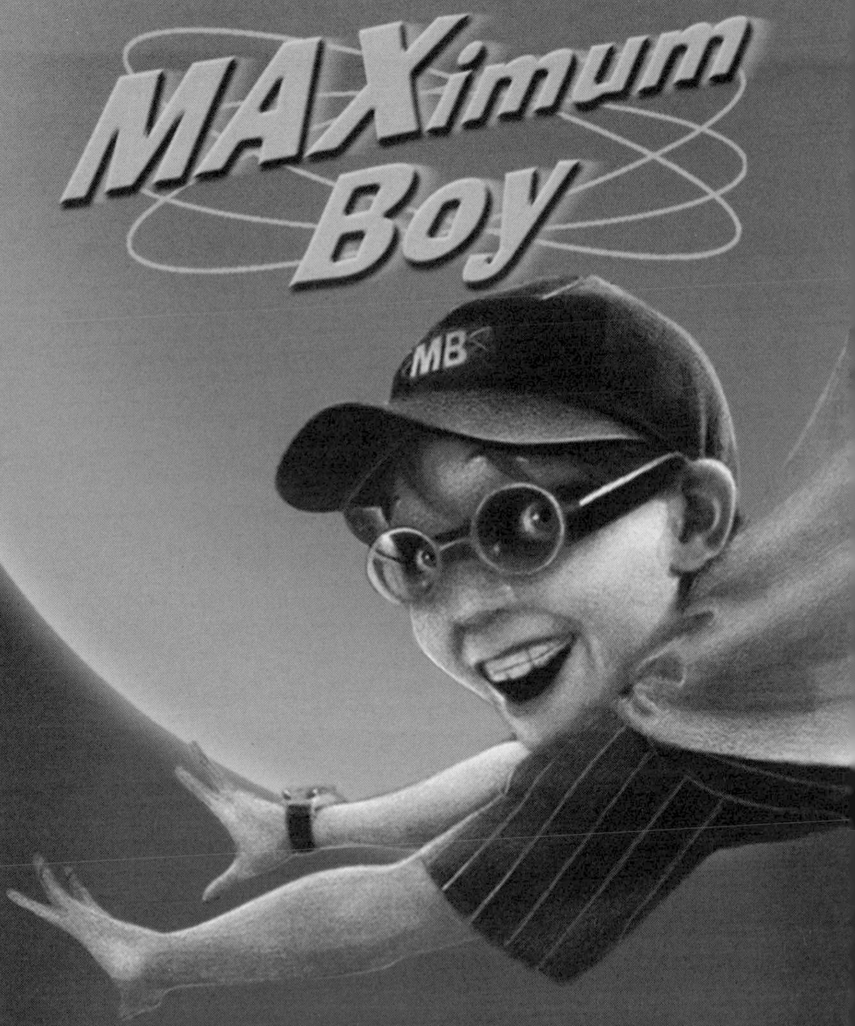
MAXimum
Boy
MB